EMMA IN THE MAGIC FOREST

INSPIRATIONAL STORIES FOR GIRLS ABOUT CONFIDENCE, COURAGE AND INNER-STRENGTH

PRESENT FOR GIRLS

Kate Bernstein

Copyright © [2021] [Kate Bernstein]

All rights reserved

The author of this book owns the exclusive right to its content.
Any commercial usage or reproduction requires the clear consent of the author.

ISBN – 9798471888524

THIS BOOK BELONGS TO

_ _ _ _ _ _ _ _ _ _ _ _ _ _ _ _ _

TABLE OF CONTENTS

EMMA AND THE NOBLE NYMPH

Emma wasn't just any ordinary child, but probably the *most* ordinary child in her neighbourhood. Most afternoons on her walk home from school, Emma would daydream of faraway lands and magical castles where she was the hero rather than a loser at school. Almost every day Emma got teased and bullied by other children for her short pixie haircut, for being the tallest girl in her class, for having an imaginative mind and even got teased when her parents divorced. She felt thoroughly unhappy and would dream every night of running away and making friends somewhere else, where no one else knew her or her problems, maybe then she might be able to catch a break.

Every day, her routine was the same: wake up, wash and have breakfast, head to school and come back home with slightly more bruises or scrapes on her shins and elbows. These bruises would appear after being pushed in the school corridors or other horrid things her classmates decided would be amusing, Emma did not find it funny. The bullying from her classmates got even worse when she told her mother, who naturally, had a meeting with the headmistress who then punished the bullies.

These bullies would then just wait until after school ended and wait for Emma on her ten-minute walk home. Feeling helpless and alone, Emma didn't know what to do other than trying to find different routes home, but each time she thought she had tricked the bullies, they would always find her.

Her kind-hearted mother was very upset when she realised how bad the bullying had become and had tried to insist that she pick Emma up from school every day. Emma refused her mothers' offer, as she knew this would mean that she would have to leave work early, pick up her baby sister from nursery before heading to Emma's school.

No, that wouldn't do at all.

Anyway, today was Friday, and Emma felt far more positive as she knew one of the bullies had to attend their weekly football club. Another was off school sick and she hoped the third kid would be put off by being the only one at school as he usually just joined in rather than instigated the confrontations. She skipped through the schools' main gates and stole a glance from side to side, expecting the usual leering faces to be approaching her from all angles.

The coast was clear.

Emma continued her walk down the main road, imagining how she would simply love to fly home on the wings of a Pegasus. She had been learning a lot about Greek mythology this term, and she had even been having super vivid dreams where she danced with nymphs, battled with satyrs and even met a Greek god! It had gripped her attention so much, on her walk home, that she didn't notice two familiar figures following behind her.

As Emma turned and followed the road around a bend, leading into a quiet part of her local suburban area, a hand gripped her shoulder, fingers digging in hard making her cry out in shock as they spun her around on the spot.

Blinking the afternoon sun out of her eyes, Emma's stomach dropped and her spirits fell as she saw two of the bullies in front of her, their grins crooked.

"Noah," Emma gasped as the taller boy took a step forward, "I thought you were at your football club tonight?" Noah stopped, ran his hand and arm over a persistently snotty nose as he laughed in her face.

"Ha! Thought you got rid of us, Phlemma?" He spat onto the ground next to Emma's shoes, his voice a high-pitched shrill as he whined Emma's nickname. The nickname 'Phlemma' had been given to the poor girl when she went to sneeze into her tissue one day, she had had a nasty cold so got teased about how much she blew her nose that day.

They never wanted to let her forget it.

Sighing, Emma shifted her bag onto her shoulders, ready to run if she needed to. The second boy stood next to Noah, he had a pale face and short black hair. Emma had always thought he looked very much like a weasel, she wanted to tell him but knew it wasn't worth the aggravation they would give her.

"So, *Phlemma*, how much money do you have on you?" Emma rolled her eyes brazenly, but anxiety began to well up inside her, she was beginning to get very anxious, as she knew what was coming.

"Noah, you know I don't have any," she retorted hotly. Noah and the pale boy both laughed together, slapping each other a high five.

"Oh yeah, that's right! Because your daddy left your mommy, and now you're poor! Waaaa!" Noah pretended to rub fake tears away from his eyes, the second boy laughing and encouraging him as Emma turned on her heel to keep walking home. Tears pricked at her eyes, and before she could stop them, the tears tumbled over her flushed cheeks, allowing everyone to see.

She hated to show them how much they upset her.

"Oh look, Iain!" Noah cried to the other boy as he chased Emma, pushing her to a stop by her shoulder. "The little girl is crying! Waaa!" The boys laughed and jeered at her, but something was stirring deep inside Emma's mind.

Emma felt a hot surge of electricity in her torso that shot out through her hands as she imagined dancing with the nymphs in her dreams.

"Leave me ALONE!" Emma bellowed, and as she turned, her index finger pointing at the smirking boys, a green light darted towards them, knocking them over.

Initially, Emma thought she had been struck by lightning, but when she realised that the sky was perfectly clear, she just stared at the boys who now were sprawled out on the ground, both faces deathly pale as they stared at her. It took Emma a second to realise that they weren't then staring at her, but the creature next to her, and Emma herself had to step back in the shock she felt.

Beside her was a young girl who glowed a pale green light, her hair was brunette but her eyes were like deep emerald gems sparkling in the sunlight. The girl turned to the two boys and took a step towards them, they tried to scramble away in horror but realised they were almost glued to the floor by an unseen force.

"Don't bully my friend Emma," the girl's voice sounded like it was echoing all around the children as if they were in a large room. "Come near her again, or tell anyone about this, you'll have to deal with me." The girl began to float a few inches into the air before the boys yelped their apologies and were finally released from the invisible hold over them, scampering away like rats. The floating girl turned to Emma, who oddly enough, was not afraid of her.

"Hello Emma, we finally meet," the girl stuck out her hand in a friendly greeting, "I'd like to be your friend. My name is Nora." Emma laughed and gripped the girl's hand firmly.

"OK Nora, I could do with a friend... but-" Emma looked in the direction that the boys had run away to, "you need to tell me what's going on?" Nora nodded and followed Emma home, explaining who she was.

Well, Emma mused, feeling more confident. *This might be the fresh start I needed.*

EMMA AND HERSELF DISCOVERY

Emma and Nora had agreed to meet early the following morning, which was a Saturday, so Emma was grateful for the break away from school and the intimidating bullies. Instead, she and Nora arranged to meet in a small glade behind Emma's house where the local lake was located in the woods. Nice and quiet for an interesting meeting. As Emma briskly walked to the glade by the lake, her stomach roiled around from anxiety, but she was also excited.

Never had anything like this ever happened to Emma, she had always been mediocre. Her grades at school, her lack of friends, her choice of clothes and even her interest in science were deemed as boring by her peers. She has always felt so dull, that she would long for something exciting to happen to her, and now it seemed like it was happening. She almost ran through the woods to get to the glade, seeing the lake to her left she took a sharp turn towards it as the strange girl had described the day before. Emma breathed in wonder as she saw open up in front of her a hidden glade, with a glorious shaft of sunlight peeking through the thick evergreen trees.

Emma stepped into the glade, peering around to see the mysterious girl, but couldn't locate her. Was this another trick conjured up by the bullies, to humiliate her away from the protection of the streets? Emma's heart quickened in pace until she heard a warm, soft voice call her name.,

"Emma, you came." Emma turned towards the voice and gasped as Nora materialised out of nowhere. Her body seemed to take on a see-through appearance for a moment, becoming solid with each step. Her dress was green and flowed in the wind, her brunette hair danced about her shoulders as Nora bounced on her toes. Her feet were bare and the soft green light still emanated from her. Emma stood, transfixed before smiling and waving.

"Nora, you said you would explain everything to me, what-" Emma was cut off as Nora giggled and held her hands, pulling her into a dance that had quick steps.

"Emma, there are so many wonderful things that you have to learn, the best way to tell you is to *show* you." Nora stopped dancing and blew a breath across the palm of her hand towards the flowers that surrounded the glade. A pale green glitter shot out from her hand, spreading across all the unopened flowers, settling upon the stems and roots glowing softly. A moment later, Emma gasped in amazement as she watched the flowers open their buds as if someone had time-lapsed a video.

"How?" Emma could only choke out one word. Nora smiled brightly.

"Magic, Emma. You have magic inside of you. You are a conjurer." Emma studied Nora's face quizzically before bursting out with laughter. Nora frowned at her rude behaviour and the young girl soon stopped, realising that her new friend was deadly serious.

"I have magic?" Nora nodded before continuing her explanation to a confused Emma.

"You are a conjurer, there are so few left of your kind because they only come into their powers when another conjurer helps them root their magic. But you rooted your own magic, Emma. Yesterday, with your determination and survival instincts, you found your power." Emma stared at her hands, trying to take in what her new friend was telling her.

"So, my power is inside of me?" Nora nodded, now kneeling on the soft grass with Emma settled beside her.

"Conjurers can create things, people and ideas from their mind," Nora tapped her head with a slim finger. Emma pointed at Nora.

"And I conjured you? If that's true, then where from? Because I don't read all that much, and I don't really like that many films. I don't recognise you from anything." Nora laughed a tinkling laugh and echoed around the glade.

"You conjured me from your dreams Emma. We don't always remember our dreams when we are awake, but sometimes when you wake up, don't you recall having a dream that felt *otherworldly*?" Nora's emerald eyes sparkled as Emma remembered this.

Tracing back the last few days, Emma had woken up each morning, thinking she was in a forest, surrounded by magic, but as her brain shook off the sleep and dreams, she forgot exactly what she had been dreaming.

Nora continued, "you need to write down your dreams, Emma. To unlock your power and potential you need to remember them as they will show you how to use your magic. You conjured me, I am a nymph, I existed only in your dreams, and now you have released me." Nora leaned in toward the stunned girl.

"But there are others in your dreams who are not kind, and who wish you harm. You need to control your magic to keep them locked away or they will cause chaos in your world." Emma nodded, but then frowned.

"So, hold up, you're a nymph that I conjured... with my mind?" The gravity of the topic began to weigh on Emma's shoulders like a heavy sack of bricks, realising there was only one of her to manage this. Nora nodded, glad that the schoolgirl was finally understanding.

"And I have the power to bring life into this world from my *dreams*? This is freaking cool!" Emma punched the air before settling back down onto the grass. Nora touched her arm gently.

"I need to teach you how to control your magic, as a master conjurer would teach you, Emma. Shall we start your training today?" Nora grinned, glad that this young girl was so thrilled to have this amazing gift. Emma bounced to her feet, excited that *finally*, she wasn't the boring, bullied girl in school anymore.

She *was* special, and she was going to move mountains. Emma felt like she could do anything and felt empowered to learn about her gift.

EMMA FINDS HER MAGIC

It had been two weeks since Emma had begun her magical training with Nora, the bullies at school had stayed away and word seemed to have spread that she was different now. Emma could now hold her head up high as she walked confidently through the school corridors, everything felt different and so right. She had even made friends with some of the girls in the library where she studied Greek mythology to find out more about Nora and what her powers were.

One day, Emma researched those nymphs were kept under control by small creatures called satyrs, a small half-man and half-goat creature who played music to the nymphs to put them under their spell to control them. Emma frowned, they didn't sound very nice, and she wondered what this small creature would look like and what sort of music it would play. For now, though, Emma would have to focus on her breathing and noting down her dreams as soon as she awoke each day.

Each evening after school and after Emma had completed her homework, Emma would work on her magic with Nora in the glade by the lake in the woods. Nora danced up to Emma, pleased to see her again.

"Today," Nora began, "we will focus on the meaning of dance!" she twirled around, her green skirts flying all about her, in her glee. Emma wrinkled her nose, she did not like dancing.

"What has dancing got to do with magic?" She huffed indignantly.

"Why, everything of course!" Nora exclaimed in surprise, she raised her hands to the light blue sky. "Dance and magic are a nymph's power, to use our magic we *must* dance. This is because magic has an ebb and flow, like water in the sea. Dancing can stir magic up and can motivate you to feel the magic inside of you." Emma sighed, rubbing the back of her neck.

"I'm not sure Nora, I have never been a good dancer," Emma shrugged as she spoke. While she felt new confidence inside of her, this was not her thing. The last time she had to dance was in the school play, and even then, she only had to walk around the stage before falling flat on her face. Nora waved her hands in the air, her eyes sparkling in the setting sun.

"Come, let us dance together. Just move your body to the sounds around you, before focusing on where you feel your magic is inside of you. Then it will make its own music for you to dance to." As she spoke, Nora began to sway her arms, jumping gracefully from side to side before pirouetting like a ballet dancer. Emma couldn't even hear any sounds that were even remotely melodic. She heard the wind, the leaves in the trees and the chitter of birds calling each other. No music in that, just noise. The young schoolgirl raised her arms anyway and began to copy Nora who stopped when she noticed.

"No, Emma, my music is different from yours, you must dance to your own sounds." Emma threw her hands into the air, exasperated.

"This is utterly ridiculous Nora, there is no music anywhere! I can't dance for toffee. There has to be another way?" Emma raised her voice as she spoke, her frustration obvious as it cut through Nora's sensitive nature like a knife through butter. Nora stopped her dance, her bottom lip trembling.

"Don't cry Nora, this is just... not me," Emma held her hands up in surrender. She felt so silly in trying to do this silly dancing business, there had to be another way. Nora's feelings were hurt by Emma's reluctance and rejection of her teachings and she hung her head, her brunette hair limp around her rather than light and floaty.

"I understand, I shall leave you be," and with that, Nora simply vanished from sight. Emma could only describe it as camouflaging into the surrounding trees, flowers and bushes until she couldn't clearly see her anymore.

"Nora, come back. I'm sorry!" Emma suddenly felt very lonely. She had been a little too critical with her words and hadn't realised that Nora was only helping her through this because she was excited to share her knowledge with the schoolgirl. Emma shook her head feeling like the bullies in her school. Her sadness overwhelmed her so much that she began to cry, her hot tears leaving small tracks over her flushed cheeks before dropping to the ground.

How could she control her magic? Shivering from the empty feeling welling up inside of her, Emma thought of a song to sing to make herself feel better. She recalled a song her mother would sing when Emma was sad and feeling lost. The tune was haunting and slow, she took deep, steadying breaths with each line of the song before holding herself up to sing a little louder before stopping in her tracks. All around her, the birds sounded as if they were singing the tune too, following her lead.

Taking another deep breath, Emma carried on, hearing different harmonies from the birds in the canopy of trees. Excitement built up inside of her, *now* she could hear music from her favourite pastime of singing. Clambering to her feet, Emma began to sing at the top of her voice, her voice was steady and in tune with the music that was now playing through her mind and she began to dance along to it.

Her dancing was different from Nora's dance, she wasn't taking large leaping steps, like a gazelle but rather lifted her hands up in the air and swayed her body around in a small circle to the rhythm of the tune.

Out of the corner of her eye, she saw Nora materialising and matched Emma's movements, complimenting them with her own style, singing along to the tune Emma purred.

Sure enough, a golden light began to swirl around Emma's hands setting off sparks all around her.

"Emma!" Nora cried, "your magic, you've got it! Oh, it's beautiful!" The golden light swirled and flowed with the song Emma sang before it blew around her like smoke in the wind as Emma finished the song.

"I did it, Nora, you helped me!" Nora blushed at Emma's words.

"Emma, you found your magic, not me. You found out that my technique doesn't work for you, but singing is your own special technique." Nora hugged her friend and Emma was glad of the comfort.

"Thank you, Nora, for believing in me," Emma whispered in the nymph's ear.

That evening Emma knew that she would have to find her own way to do things, no matter how hard it might be or how long it might take. She couldn't copy other people's ideas and knew she would have to work harder on her magic.

EMMA AND THE GREEDY SATYR

Emma worked tirelessly on her singing magic, she would sing in her room the last thing of an evening and loved watching the golden glow around her hands wash through her. It tasted like butter and smelt like caramel the more she used it, the magic was delicious.

One night, Emma slept, tossing from side to side from a nightmare. She dreamt that a mean-looking satyr was trying to get her to betray Nora, and tell him of Nora's location. Emma refused to tell him before sitting bolt upright and yelling out. Her golden magic shot out from her fingertips as she reached forward in her bed. The dream had been so vivid she had to take a deep breath. Glancing over to her open bedroom window she saw the outline of a strange shape. It looked like the outline of the satyr from her dream, but as she rubbed her eyes and stared back at the window it was gone.

Great, Emma thought, *now I'm having waking dreams*. Quickly scribbling into her dream journal the issue of the waking dream, Emma tiptoed to the kitchen to get some water before heading back to bed and burying herself back under the sheets.

The following day was the end of the weekend and Emma handed her dream journal to Nora who checked it for anything that might help with Emma's magic. Nora stopped on the final page from when Emma had noted down her waking dream.

"A waking dream?" Nora whispered, looking a little pale and stared back at the young girl. "What did you see?" Emma shrugged.

"Well, I've been doing some research on you and who you are." Emma blushed a deep pink in her cheeks. She didn't want Nora to think she didn't trust her, but Nora blushed herself a little and smiled, apparently grateful for the thought.

When Emma informed Nora that she saw what she thought was the shape of a satyr in her bedroom window after she woke up from a frightening dream about him, Nora's face pinched.

"Emma," Nora's voice was low and trembling. "What you saw was real. You've been working on your magic so well that you conjured a satyr in your sleep." Emma raised an eyebrow.

"Oh, what does that mean though? You look worried." Emma frowned at the concerned look on her friend's face. Nora wrung her hands together in worry.

"Satyrs are evil, Emma." The word evil hit Emma like a punch in her gut. "Satyrs capture nymphs and use their powers for their own use. He will be after me, and if I hear his music I will not be able to resist it." Emma shook her head. No, there had to be a way around it.

"How do I put him back, Nora? Or capture him?" Emma was determined not to let her friend be taken by a wicked creature that *she* had summoned, it would eat her up inside.

"You can trap him inside your mind forever, but you'll need to be careful not to release him again." Emma nodded, agreeing that she could manage that and they should set to work tracking the satyr.

Just then, Emma heard a hauntingly beautiful piece of music that seemed to envelop her and Nora. Nora gasped as she heard it, holding Emma's gaze.

"He's here," was all the nymphs could say before she began to dance, her eyes blank and her face in a forced smile. Emma looked all around, there was no one place that the haunting melody was coming from, it sounded like it was all around her.

Emma began to sing her song and as she felt the magic stir up inside of her, she sensed the magic of the music. The music came from a tree, and Emma let her golden magic swirl all around the tree trunk, scanning it before realising that the tree *was* the satyr.

Bringing her magic from the pit of her stomach, Emma punched the tree with a swipe of magic and out from the trunk fell the outline of the creature Emma had seen the night before. Lying on the ground of the glade wood sat a fat man with goat legs and a set of panpipes in his hands. He scrambled to his cloven hooves and began to play a different tune, one that was even slower and made Emma feel sleepy. Before she could stop herself, her legs gave way and her head spun in circles as sleep overcame her.

The satyr had lulled her to sleep with his pipes, and now she knew how powerful his music was, she had to get the pipes away from him. Sleep had overcome Emma but disappeared as quickly as it had arrived as the satyr turned his attention to the nymph who was trying to transform into a tree, so he couldn't capture her.

Emma clambered to her feet and knew she must act quickly before he turned on her again. Humming to herself to regain her magic, the warm golden glow soon turned into a cloud and as Emma moved her hand sharply as if to hit the satyr, a golden bolt of lightning emanated from the cloud, striking the satyr's panpipes. The wooden pipes shattered into tiny pieces, splinters shot into the ground and Nora was pulled out of the satyr's magical grip.

"Emma, you did it! You broke his panpipes!" The satyr squealed and hollered, sounding like he was half bleating like a goat and shouting like a person.

"How dare you!" He shouted and bleated at Emma, "to interfere with the sacred work of a satyr!" Emma quietened down his noisy protests with a wave of her golden cloud, the satyr whimpered and cowered away.

"Who are you?" Emma demanded. The satyr pulled himself up to his full height of three feet.

"I am Sidneous, Sid for short." Emma crossed her arms across her chest as she glared at the short creature.

"Well, Sid. Nora is my friend. And I am not going to let you hurt her or take her anywhere. She is a free nymph." The satyr snorted down a wide nose that almost looked like a snout.

"She won't be for long, I have called on my people. They will make their way here and take her. Her magic is very powerful, we will have her!" Nora quailed in fear as the satyr pointed in her direction.

Emma raised her hands to banish the satyr back into her mind, but the satyr saw the movement and dashed away into the woods, squealing and bleating. Looking defeated Emma glanced over to Nora.

"What now?" Nora walked up to her friend and patted her shoulders.

"Now we conjure backup. We need to get people on our side. Sid told the truth: he called for more satyrs, so you need to conjure up some more powerful beings to help us fight in the final battle."

Emma's mind spun around for a little before she began her calming breathing exercises.

The schoolgirl was young and had plenty of growing up to do, but she knew she could do it. After all, look at how much she had accomplished already. She had broken a magical creature's power source, this was something she had heard about only in books and films!

Puffing out her chest and slapping high five with Nora Emma knew she could do it, she just needed to train her magic more to gain more control while she slept. Emma felt that she was strong enough to do anything.

EMMA EXPLORES HER SLEEP STATE

"Hey, Emma!" Emma stopped abruptly in her tracks, her feet barely over the line of concrete that defined the school front playground with the pavement on the main road. She almost made it without any trouble. Sighing and shifting the weight of her school bag on her shoulders, Emma slowly turned and glared at the boys who had bullied her relentlessly for years.

While it was true that they hadn't bothered her for a few weeks, Emma's confidence wavered as they swaggered up to her, dropping their bags and cracking their knuckles as they approached. There was no way Emma could use her magic in front of the school, then everyone would know and she would never hear the end of it. That also meant they wouldn't touch her as the teacher stood guard, eyeing up the groups of children that clustered together to say their goodbyes to each other.

The boys now surrounded her on all sides, but Emma kept calm.

"Where's your freaky friend Emma? She left and abandoned you?" Noah stepped forward, hair flopping into his eyes which he scraped at with his fingers.

"Oh no," Emma replied coolly, "I'm due to meet her here soon, right there." She pointed to the outside part of the school gate, and the boys nervously looked around. Emma turned, her head tilted to one side and a large grin crept across her face. She knew they were frightened of Nora, so Emma thought the best thing to do is to play into that fear.

"But *she* isn't the one you want to worry about." Noah glared at Emma before barking a laugh in her face. Before Noah realised what happened, Emma used a gust of wind mixed in with her magic to trip Noah up and the boy fell flat on his face.

"What the-" Scrambling to his feet Noah then ran away.

"Come on lads, she's not worth our time." He rubbed his nose and as he turned away Emma clicked her fingers at him, shooting out a small tendril of gold, too small to see with the naked eye. The tendrils hit him square on his shoulder blade and Noah yelped and ran, his sidekicks running with him.

Laughing to herself all the way home to the glade wood Emma felt a sense of power, she wouldn't let bullies upset her anymore. She wouldn't let herself be the victim, the new Emma would stand and fight.

Seeing Nora dancing in the glade filled Emma's heart with joy and she ran to her friend, singing with her as Nora spun her emerald magic into the air.

Once the pair stopped for breath, Nora turned to Emma, a grave look on her face.

"Emma, last night you spun your magic in your sleep. The more powerful you get, the stronger the creatures you release from your dreams." Emma's face fell, what had she done?

"Who else is free?" Nora shook her head at Emma's question.

"Not free, trapped. Another nymph, Nellie, is trapped by a satyr who you released out into the real world, but she is trapped eternally in your Sleep State. She needs to be freed or she'll be trapped forever."

Emma frowned. "But if it's in my sleep state then it's not real?" Nora shook her head.

"We are real, to you, in your mind. But as you were sleeping last night you accidentally released another satyr who was tracking Nellie in your dreams. He managed to trap her because the line between dream and reality was blurred, making it possible for him to trap her. We need to free her into this world, and to do that you need to sleep." Emma knew what she had to do, and she laid down on the soft grass, Nora's magic swirled around her and a soft lullaby played in the clearing as it pulled Emma into a lucid dream.

The world dropped away from Emma and she found herself standing in the middle of the woods. Glad to know the woods like the back of her hand, Emma built up her magic and began to cast out tendrils of golden magic to sense where Nellie was.

Soon enough, Emma found her and she began to run in the direction, never feeling as though she were running. Emma began to pant when suddenly, the ground gave way and she fell, her stomach churning from the sudden drop but soon enough Emma was back on her feet standing in front of a large cage, made up of vines from the trees. Inside was a girl in a pastel yellow dress, sobbing and Emma walked up to her. The girl jerked her head up, her hair was gold like the sun and light bounced off the top of her head.

"Who are you?" Emma raised her hands to calm the young girl, she looked to be about 10 years old, but Emma knew that nymphs didn't age, they were born with the earth.

"I am Emma, I am here to release you from this cage." The girl smiled and the golden yellow of her hair and face shone brightly.

"Emma!" She breathed as if she knew the schoolgirl well. Standing back from the cage, Emma hummed to herself and built up the magic in her hands. She targeted the cage tendrils and shot the golden light, it sizzled from the impact on the cage and the vines retreated back into the shadows of the trees until Emma and Nellie stood alone.

"Come with me," Emma didn't know exactly what to do, but she held out her hand to the young-looking nymph, nodding reassuringly. As soon as Nellie gripped Emma's hand a white light burst across Emma's vision and she found herself lying on her back in the middle of the woods with Nora looking over her, beaming.

"You did it, Emma!" Nora helped Emma sit up and she saw Nellie standing nearby, half hiding in a bush. Seeing Emma standing, Nellie danced forward, her bright yellow glow shone throughout the glade.

"You saved me! Thank you, Emma!" Nora cleared her throat.

"We still have to track down the satyr though. Emma, he is a powerful one. Do you think you're up for the task?" Emma grinned and nodded.

"I can definitely do it." After everything Emma had learned recently, she knew her capabilities had no limits. It was no one else who saved Nellie, but she knew without Nora's help she wouldn't have come as far as she had in her abilities. Despite the odds of a powerful satyr having been released, Emma knew she had to try, and try she would.

Nothing was going to stop Emma from reaching her potential, from doing good and helping these wonderful magical people. Feeling confident that she was gaining more of her powers Emma, Nora and Nellie began to make their plan to capture the satyr.

EMMA HELPS A TINY FRIEND

The following day after school, Nellie and Nora began to help Emma to unlock the ability to wilfully conjure an object from her Sleep State by meditating and focusing on the object.

Emma sat down on the grass; the two nymphs sat on either side of her to support her if she needed their magic. As Emma breathed in deeply, she saw in her mind a pen that she thought would be a good test of her abilities. Building up the magic in her hands and humming a low tune, Emma made the golden magic hover around the pen and pulled it towards her, until she held it in her hand. The pen felt heavy, metallic as the girl pulled the lid off to inspect it. She couldn't believe that she was meditating in her Sleep State, where people had their dreams and she was able to command herself to do certain things without losing control. It was amazing and Emma felt absolutely exhilarated.

As Emma woke up, she looked in her hand and there lay the pen innocently sparkling in the afternoon sun. It weighed the same and it still had a smooth metallic finish to it.

Nora patted her on her back.

"Do you think you could conjure a live object now?" She asked Emma. The shy girl hesitated before nodding and crossed her legs again, slowing down her breathing until she was back in her Sleep State.

In her imagination, she saw a small creature, tiny in fact. The creature had a tiny figure, covered in flower petals and long shimmering gossamer wings protruded from its back.

It was a fairy, Emma gasped at how beautiful it was, the tiny face was surrounded by a shock of green moss that looked like it could be hair. The creature opened its eyes, which almost took up all of the space on its face and the creature beamed at Emma as she held out her hand. The same white light shone brightly and Emma was soon eager to see the creature she had brought forth from her Sleep State.

The fairy was the same beautiful-looking creature that she saw in her mind, and it hovered in the air, its gossamer wings flapping like a hummingbird's wings.

"Hello," the fairy squeaked, "I am Allette, I've been waiting to meet you, Emma." The tiny fairy flew about the space in front of Emma, but all Emma could see was a small bright glow, like a firefly. Allette was too fast to see, so she settled on Emma's knee.

"You saved me, Emma. I was being hunted down in your dreams by a wicked sorcerer." Allette's tiny face creased with concern. "I am worried he will come here, he is not bound by your Sleep State as he has his own magic. He is evil!" Emma frowned and looked at Nora.

"What do you know about sorcerers Nora?" Nora frowned in concern and shrugged.

"From what I have seen, sorcerers are just selfish, wanting magic for themselves. But they're easily pleased and it would be easy to persuade him that he doesn't need a fairy's magic." Emma frowned.

"But Allette said he's evil?" Emma knew there was so much more history to this magical world she was unlocking, and it would take time to understand it all. Nora shook her head.

"Not evil, just arrogant. We should wait for him to come for Allette, and then deal with him then."

So, the nervous fairy, confident nymphs and the fledgling conjurer all waited, playing games to pass the time. As the sorcerer drew nearer the fairy flitted anxiously from person to person, seeking a little comfort from everyone, accidentally dropping her fairy dust as she flew.

Soon enough, a loud CRACK sounded in the air and a lightning bolt slammed into the ground, making everyone jump. From the smoke stood a tall man with a long flowing cloak.

"Good evening," he bowed theatrically, "I am Blaze, a fire sorcerer. I have tracked down the magic scent of a fairy that is meant to be under my domain..." Blaze searched the small group before spotting the tiny fairy quivering in Emma's coat that lay over a tree branch.

"Aha! There she is!" Blaze exclaimed before dancing from foot to foot, creating a cage in his hands. Nora and Emma scrambled to their feet and Emma stepped forward deftly, putting herself in the way. Remembering Nora's words about him being arrogant Emma smiled at him.

"Why is such a powerful sorcerer like you, searching for a tiny fairy?" Blaze puffed out his chest, pride swelling up inside. He swished his long hair over his shoulder grinning at the young girl before inhaling deeply toward her.

"Ah, a young fledgling conjurer, glad of it - the world needs more folk like you! Well as you ask my dear girl, that fairy is a source of magic for me." Emma pretended to look confused and walked over to Allette, holding her up by her wings. Allette froze and stared in horror - what was Emma doing?

"But this tiny fairy doesn't have all that much magic-" The sorcerer cut Emma off mid-sentence.

"That's where you would be wrong! If I absorb her power, it will enhance my own!" Blaze held out the small cage he had created moments earlier. Emma shook her head.

"But I can sense that your magic is double the size of this fairy, Mr. Blaze. Her magic wouldn't hold a candle to your power!" Emma's tone sounded so genuine that Blaze halted and made eye contact with the girl.

"You really think so?" He asked, astonished. Emma nodded fervently.

"Oh yes, part of my gift is sensing the magic of others, and I can tell that her magic is not as great as yours. You don't need this insignificant creature!" Emma released Allette's wings and the fairy just hovered in the air, unsure whether to be happy or offended. Blaze strutted around the glade, his chest puffed out bigger than ever and he ran his hair through his fingers.

"No, I guess not. Why thank you, my dear girl. You have opened my eyes!" Emma bowed her head.

"Glad I could be of service, Master." At her words Blaze grinned and with a SWOOSH of his cloak, he disappeared in a puff of smoke.

The magical creatures all turned to Emma, their mouths hanging open and Allette hugged Emma's shoulder.

"Thank you, Emma," she squeaked, "although you were wrong, fairy magic is super strong! I'm glad you convinced him!" Nora and Nellie laughed.

"Well, I wasn't going to let you get kidnapped on my watch!" Emma laughed and high-fived the tiny fairy with her finger.

"I'll repay you in any way you need Emma, name it!" Emma grinned at the fairy's offer.

"Well, we sort of need to build a magical army to take down a satyr. What do you say?" Allette squealed in excitement.

"Fairy magic would be perfect for such a task! I shall go inform my people, maybe we can all help you!" And with that, Allette sped away into the setting sun.

Feeling good about herself, Emma knew that this was what she was supposed to do with her life. Helping magical creatures, keeping them safe and making new friends was heart-warming and fulfilling. Emma knew then that the sorcerer wasn't evil, as Nora had said. Some people are just misunderstood and need a little push in the right direction. She knew that she shouldn't even judge someone by how they look, but by the things they do and words they say.

EMMA HELPS FIX MAGIC

Emma practiced her magic every single day, until one day she was so tired that she flopped onto her back one evening in the middle of the glade as Nellie and Nora both danced their Nature magic. Emma watched the pair of nymphs as they danced and glided around the clearing, the sun sparkled through the trees and the lake glittered reflections all around the three individuals. It was so peaceful; Emma didn't want this moment to end.

However, she was getting bored, she didn't feel like she was learning anything new and now it was the summer holidays there was no schoolwork to take the edge off her boredom. Her parents seemed pleased to see Emma outside in the fresh air. Emma would smirk to herself as she made her way to the glade - if only her parents knew what she could really do!

Turning to Nora, Emma groaned at her graceful friend who spun green smoke between her hands, flowers blooming all around her, the leaves on the trees growing darker and larger.

"Nora, is there anyone who I could... I don't know... *teach* my magic to?" Both the nymphs stopped in their tracks, their magic exploding as they lost their focus to gaze at Emma.

Nora grinned and said, "Emma, are you getting The Call?" The young girl shrugged in response, unsure as to what The Call even was.

"I don't know, what is *The Call?*" I asked. Nellie squealed and clapped her hands together in excitement as Nora cleared her throat.

"The Call is when a conjurer feels the need to pass on their magic to others. And Nellie and I actually do know some creatures who need some magic to protect them from the satyrs." Emma knelt beside Nora peering up into her face.

"Is there a serious problem with the satyrs Nora?" Emma asked, her hands held tensely in her lap. Nora just sighed as Nellie weaved flowers through her own hair, weaving the delicate stems through her hair as she and Emma listened to Nora.

"The satyrs are after power, Emma. Mine and Nellie's power, the fairies' power... even your power." A shiver ran down Emma's spine. Why would anyone want something that belonged to someone else?

"But why?" Emma asked. Nora sighed.

"Satyrs are very greedy, like little pigs always wanting more than they already have. Emma, you could teach others to protect themselves and tap into their natural magic. Gnomes, trolls and pixies can do magic, but the ones I know aren't able to use theirs as it's been stolen! You have to help them, Emma." Nodding Emma stood to her feet.

"I want to help; how can I start?" Nora grabbed Emma's hand and the three girls ran together, Nora and Nellie leading Emma deeper into the woods until they came upon the other side of the lake.

As the three stepped through a curtain of ivy and moss they saw a large clearing in front of them and hundreds of magical creatures and people were gathered, dancing, knitting, reading, singing and playing music together.

"How did I not ever see this?" Emma gasped as she gazed around the clearing. These creatures all moved together in harmony and they didn't notice the newcomer as she felt like she stuck out like a sore thumb. Nora danced into the middle of the clearing and clapped her hands. All the creatures quieted and gazed at Nora as she explained her presence.

"Creatures and magical people, I stand here to announce that my friend, Emma the Conjurer, would like to teach some of you how to use your magic that the satyrs stole! Raise your hands if you are interested!" Emma breathed out in amazement as all the creatures' hands were raised into the air.

"You all want *me* to teach you? But I'm just a kid!" Nora shook her head.

"Emma, you're so much more than a kid. You have conjured some of these creatures from your dreams over the years, the rest other untrained conjurers around the world have conjured. So, we all gather here, to stay safe. But some of us need your help. Here-" She bounded over to Emma, taking her hand before pulling her eagerly towards a group of dwarves.

"These dwarves are meant to have the ability to find lost and hidden treasure which they use for its energy, these gnomes here," again she pulled Emma away from the small men and tugged her towards a small group of what Emma thought were miniature figurines with tiny little hats on. "These gnomes are supposed to help keep the balance of nature, working with us nymphs. Everyone in some way needs help Emma, are you able to be that person?" Emma straightened up and nodded firmly.

"Yes, I will help these people." She clenched her fist in determination and nodded her head beaming, finally, she had a purpose.

Emma went to help the gnomes first, showing them how to meditate to tap into their power and before long, they found that they could tap into their power whenever they felt like it. The gnomes were able to focus on the task they wanted to complete, whether it's digging up worms or fixing holes in nests, the gnomes found their power by concentrating hard on what they needed to do to keep the balance of nature.

Moving onto the dwarves, Emma helped them find their own power by special breathing techniques and imaging their treasure in their mind, able to draw power from the pretend gems and coins in their head until they could find the real thing.

All the creatures and people that Emma was helping made her feel happy, she felt good that she was giving back to others and felt this was what she was meant to do.

Soon it was time for Emma to go home and get ready for bed. As she snuggled into her comfortable bed, she giggled to herself. No one would ever believe how amazing her life was, frolicking with nymphs, finding treasure with real dwarves and using *magic*! She felt good about herself, knowing that she could finally help others made her feel positive and confident. Emma never wanted this feeling to go, not even for her to sleep!

EMMA AND THE MESSENGER GOD

The day that Nellie and Nora thought that Emma should test her powers further was a warm, sunny day. Emma had been working on her powers in her sleep state, so she wouldn't conjure anything or anyone accidentally, as by now she had conjured quite a few creatures and animals from trolls to rabbits. She had finally stopped having these dreams where she couldn't control her magic, but now she was very well rehearsed and could control herself and so the two young nymphs suggested to her that she should conjure a powerful being in her sleep state.

"Emma," Nora began as the sun shone high in the sky. "Nellie, me and the other creatures need your protection from the satyr that had tried to trap me, we have heard he has joined forces with other satyrs who are planning to capture us. If you can conjure one powerful being then we will be able to fight!" Emma felt deflated.

"But I don't think I can do that, what if something goes wrong?" Emma asked her friends. Nora smiled a little and held Emma's small hands in her own.

"We will be right beside you. True friends never leave each other in difficult situations. We will be here to support you. Emma, you are the most powerful conjurer I have ever had the pleasure of meeting - you can do this. You are strong!" As Nora spoke, Emma felt more confident with each word, her heartbeat a little faster and she held her head up high, nodding.

"OK, let's do this." Emma declared.

Lying down on her back in a comfortable position, Emma focussed on her breathing and soon the familiar floating sensation overcame her and before long she knew she was in her sleep state.

Opening her eyes Emma saw she was where she had been lying on the soft grass in the clearing, there seemed to be a green light filtering through the tree branches, shining through the clearing. Following the green light, Emma eventually came upon a lagoon that she knew was not in the waking world. Emma knew these parts of the woods really well and so she understood that this lagoon only existed in her sleep state. She stood at the edge of the lagoon, a short waterfall crashed down on the other side of the unusually calm waters beside a large boulder.

Daintily sitting on top of the boulder was a man with short golden curls that shifted gently in the breeze, playing a gold lyre that sat across his lap, plucking at the strings creating a beautiful calm tune.

Emma watched, entranced by the beauty of his music, and sighed as the music drifted all around her. The melody danced around her mind and Emma sensed with her magic this man's abilities. She could sense he was strong, and his magic had a lot of capability in the waking world.

Carefully stepping into the water Emma knew she had to make contact and as she stepped further into the water she noticed the water felt like silk rather than a wet sensation.

"Hello Emma," the man cooed from his lofty perch. The music stopped and the two stared at each other, Emma smiling but he just stared back unsmiling.

"Why do you think I can help you?" The blonde man said. Emma shrugged.

"My magic brought me to you, I trust it with my life. You have to be the one to help us." The man leaned forward with a frown on his face.

"What makes you think I *want* to help you?" He challenged her, the corner of his mouth flickering up into a sneer. Emma knew that she would have to find out who he was, and so letting her magic flow from her she closed her eyes, breathing in steadily.

Sensing more about him, her magic answered some of her questions.

"You're Hermes, the messenger god. Protector of travellers, nature creatures and nymphs." The man nodded and grinned.

"You have good control over your abilities, Emma." Emma inclined her head in thanks before continuing.

"Hermes, we need your help. My friends are nymphs, and they are in danger by some satyrs who are looking to kidnap them and steal their magic. Please, we need your protection." Hermes ruffed his thick blonde curls and sighed, leaning back onto his opposite arm on the boulder, pondering the question.

"I cannot help you, Emma, I am of no use to anyone anymore," he shook his head, defeated. Emma stepped forward, fixing him with a fierce glare.

"Please, Hermes. We need your protection. I can only do so much, I haven't yet mastered my conjuring powers, but you can protect my friends. You are the smartest god I could think of, the only one strong enough to defeat these evil satyrs. You did it once before..." her voice trailed off. Then Emma had an idea.

"If you won't take *my* word for it, let me show you." She waded through the silky waters and settled her thumb onto Hermes' forehead to connect her magic to his magic. She didn't know why she was doing this, she just knew deep inside that this would work.

As soon as she touched his head, she imagined her friends, the woodland creatures she had conjured, her own magical ability journey and the nymphs she had befriended. Emma sensed that Hermes was feeling sad, and emotional at her plea and as they disconnected he fixed her gaze with electric blue eyes.

"Alright, I shall come back with you, young conjurer. I will do what I can." Emma's heart soared and so she held his hands before bringing herself and him back through to the waking world.

Opening her eyes, she took in Hermes' face in the glade and he smiled before leaning away from her. He looked around at the nymphs and other magical creatures who flocked to him, bowing before him.

Nora danced with Nellie with joy and embraced Emma in a tight hug.

"Emma, you did it! You conjured a god! A god of nature and nymphs, how did you know?" Emma shrugged.

"My magic led me to him," Emma responded simply.

Emma stepped back and watched everyone celebrating around her and Hermes, glad that they had someone who could help back them up. Emma realised that she finally did something amazing that she didn't think she could do, she had doubted herself in conjuring someone so powerful.

Feeling proud of herself Emma joined her friends in their celebration. This was going to be amazing, she just knew it.

EMMA AND THE FINAL BATTLE

The following day Emma felt tense, Nora had told her that the satyrs were close to where they were based in the wood by the lake and they were trying to find the weak points in their camp to try to kidnap them. Hermes had suggested that Emma bait the satyrs, as the goat-men hadn't yet seen him with the nymphs, it would be a big surprise for them.

"Emma, I agree with Hermes. Baiting the satyrs will be the easiest thing to do, but we aren't sure how to do it." Nora wrung her hands together, nervous about what to do. Emma thought for a moment and turned to Hermes.

"I think the nymphs need to appear alone but have you close by to capture the satyrs so I can banish them back to my sleep state." Emma turned back to the nervous nymphs. "What do you think?" Nellie stepped forward and nodded in response to Emma's question.

"I think it's a good plan, let's do it." With that, they set to work. The magical creatures all hid under bushes and used their magic to hide in plain sight. The two nymphs moved towards the lakeside, finding a nice quiet bank to wash and groom themselves in, knowing that the water would trap them if the satyrs tried to flank them. This was all part of Emma's plan, and Hermes created a boulder to hide behind.

It took time for the satyrs to find the nymphs, but as Emma and the other creatures stayed hidden, and Nellie and Nora stayed out in the open the satyrs couldn't resist attempting to trap them. From her hiding place, Emma watched the satyrs come into view, the nymphs pretended they didn't see them approaching.

Breathing in sharply, Emma counted ten satyrs... that was a lot of magical creatures. Her confidence faltered and suddenly she felt like that victim in front of the bullies, feeling paralysed by fear. What if she couldn't do this? Her friends would be captured and she would be alone, unable to help them.

No, she couldn't let herself feel like this. She had to stay focused and she imagined Nellie and Nora's happy, smiling faces in her mind. The fairies, trolls and other magical creatures she helped save over the last few weeks she imagined were frolicking in the woods, splashing in the lake waters and feeling safe. That's what she wanted more than anything for her friends, was to feel safe.

Once she saw the satyrs in place, she stood on the spot-on cue and shouted at them

"Hey, Billy Goat-Gruff, what are you doing trip-trapping over my bridge?" Her voice echoed all around her as she shouted at the angry-looking satyrs. The satyrs stared at her, snarling as they began to step towards her. Each satyr was a different height, some were taller, others were fat and their fur varied from brown to gold and chestnut.

Seeing so many of these creatures and she didn't know what they were capable of.

Not letting fear take hold of her, Emma made a high-pitched whistle and as she did so Hermes appeared in a cloud of smoke.

The satyrs gasped in shock as they saw Hermes appear before them, they froze in fear. Hermes raised his lyre and began to play, the music taking hold of all the satyrs, preventing them from running away.

"Emma," Hermes called, "banish them." Emma walked forward, Nellie and Nora by her side with their hands on her shoulders as she conjured her magic and cast it around each satyr, banishing them and locking them all back into her sleep state, one by one.

The last satyrs to be banished was Sid, he let out a howl of anguish as Emma's magic forced him back inside her sleep state, never to be let out again.

Using so much magic in such a short space of time, tired Emma out and she fell to her knees, taking deep breaths to steady herself. As she calmed down, she realised she could hear cheering and looking up she saw the clearing filling with the magical creatures she had conjured and befriended.

She did it, she couldn't believe it, but she actually did it! Emma's friends lifted her on their shoulders, cheering for *her*! Tears filled Emma's eyes as feelings of confidence and worthiness filled her heart.

"I did it," she whispered. "I DID it!" Whooping for joy Emma pumped her fist into the air.

It was at that point that Emma knew she could do anything that she wanted to. She didn't need to be scared or worried about what her peers would think of her, she had learned to love herself and Emma felt empowered to be able to manage on her own in the waking world. Feeling happy and content, Emma danced right into the evening with her friends, confident in her new abilities.

DISCLAIMER

This book contains opinions and ideas of the author and is meant to teach the reader informative and helpful knowledge while due care should be taken by the user in the application of the information provided. The instructions and strategies are possibly not right for every reader and there is no guarantee that they work for everyone. Using this book and implementing the information/recipes therein contained is explicitly your own responsibility and risk. This work with all its contents, does not guarantee correctness, completion, quality, or correctness of the provided information. Misinformation or misprints cannot be completely eliminated.